INDHUMATHI

LOHIT CHANDU

"*Dedicated*

To,

All the Indian girls,

Who dares to dream."

Contents

NOTION PRESS PUBLICATIONS

presents

"I N D H U M A T H I PaperBack Version"

Amazon Kindle Publications

presents

"I N D H U M A T H I E -Version"

Acknowledgements

"Hello Readers,

I use the old-fashioned term to address you, because I like it and because I know that only the gentler kind of person is likely to care much for my stories

I have never been any good at the more brilliant sort of writing, But I preferred to write about the people and their places.

Perhaps there is too much of me in my stories, and at times my books may read like an autobiography. It is a weakness, I know. It can't be helped; I am that kind of a writer, that kind of a person.

I am happier being this type of writer. But this book is completely different.

It's a story of a girl named Indhumathi. The book starts with a backward urging the reader to read the middle chapter first before deciding to go ahead with the book. The book is all about a girl how she survives in her life after her marriage breakdown. This book follows the most exciting years in Indhumathi's Life - early childhood to late teens. The story is quite imaginative and sensitive. This is a memorable story about small lives in Sarangi Nagar with all the hallmarks of classic prose.

LOHIT CHANDU
1-05-2022."

About The Book

"

It's a story of a girl named Indhumathi. The book starts with a backward urging the reader to read the middle chapter first before deciding to go ahead with the book. The book is all about a girl how she survives in her life after her marriage breakdown. This book follows the most exciting years in Indhumathi's Life - early childhood to late teens. The story is quite imaginative and sensitive. This is a memorable story about small lives in Sarangi Nagar with all the hallmarks of classic prose.
"

Preface

"Well, *most of the people were good at expressing their emotions, talking freely with others, and faking with others. I'm not really any one of them. I'm sitting in front of the mirror running a comb through my long black hair. The dressing table was crowded with all kinds of lotions, mascaras, paints, oil and Moisturizers. I looked at my room, it was untidy and my bed was full of my new sarees lay draped with chains and jewelry. The hall is full of relatives, yes, I am going to get married in the next couple hours.*

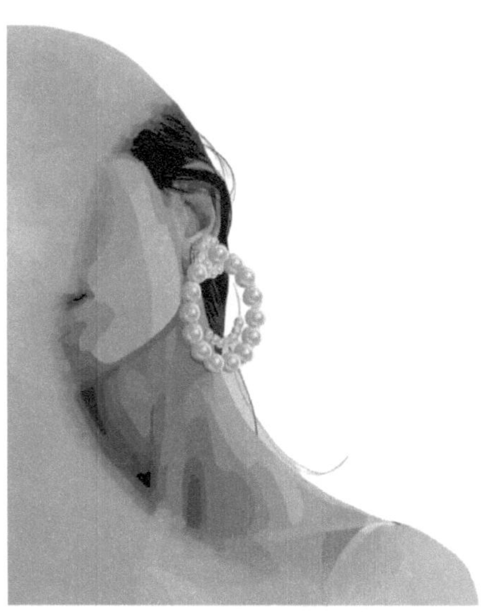

”

ONE
CHAPTER-1

Go, take a bath and come fast. It's already late. I'll wait here, said Sunitha. No wait Sunitha let me take my new sky blue lehenga...I said.

Wow it's really beautiful, is this are you wearing for the reception now? Sunitha asked curiously looking at the lehenga. Yes, how's it? I asked Wow, it's really awesome she replied. Hmm, Sunitha can you please take the matching necklace that I kept in the 2nd zip of my suitcase I said and went to the restroom for bathing. I undressed myself and walked closer to the mirror. I saw my body and a voice from inside me said

I would be standing naked in front of a new man very soon. I fastly took a shower and came out rolling a towel to my body. In the meantime, Mohini aunty came to the room and started shouting beta,

Come fast it's already late. The bridegroom was already at the stage and the groom's relatives were waiting to see

you. She said and continued Sunitha beta. Please help her to get dressed and left from that place.

Mohini Aunt was my father's sister. She was a strong woman. Her voice was warm and deep, her face was a happy one.

Sunitha locked the room and I unrolled the towel from my body and attached my skinny inners to my private parts. ***A woman with a bra on her breasts and panties between her legs will obviously look sexier***. I wore my new lehenga and sat opposite to the mirror and Sunitha started polishing me to look beautiful and my voice from inside started shouting Come on Indhu, cheer up finally you are going to step into the next phase of your life!

Hi, I am Indhumathi and I am getting married today. I am twenty-four years old. I was born in a small village and grew up in Sarangi Nagar. Before you are going to read my story let me warn you. You may not like me too much. Because I'm scared of little things, I hate comparison with others and most importantly I wear sleeveless T-shirts and torn jeans.

My mother had married a Government Teacher, she died while I was still a baby. My father himself was not a strong man, and fought with tuberculosis while bringing me up. He never left me alone up to my sixth birthday. That day he found he was having tuberculosis. My father, who is supposed to sleep with me, started sleeping in another room and for the first time I started feeling lonely in my entire life. My father noticed my loneliness and she decided to send me to her sister's place for my higher studies.

One day in the middle of the night, without my being aware of it, I woke up to experience, for a day, all the terrors of abandonment. Yes, it was Mohini Aunt that Insert chapter one text here. day she arrived at my house. She took me with her to her flat in Sarangi Nagar and I thought this ***'small flat was to be my home for the next couple of years'*** I thought. The age of six is the beginning of an interesting period in the girl's life, and the months I spent with Aunt

Mohini are not difficult to recall but the hardest part with her is she had a habit of comparing people with others. She had a husband whose name is Ram Murthy. I used to call him uncle Ram. He works in a furniture shop which is very close to his house. Aunt Mohini was a joyous, bubbling creature and every time I think of her, I am tempted by her magnificent physique. She had long arms and broad thighs. She was majestic, and at the same time she was graceful. Above all, she was warm and full of understanding, and it was this tenderness of hers that overcame resentment and jealousy in other women. There was a balcony in the room. I always stand there to see people. There were a number of children playing in the road, and they all stared at me. They must have wondered what my dark, black-haired aunt was doing with a strange child who was fairer than most.

Aunt Mohini's rooms were untidy compared with the neatness of my house in my village. My friend Sunitha and I go to school every day. Sunitha is one and only best friend. As I was living far from my father and had no mother, I used to share my every feeling with her. She was the most important person in my life. In Fact, I used to talk to myself more until Sunitha came into my life. In school days Sunitha had more crushes on her, Infact she is the boy's girl. The actual problems in my life started at the age of 16 when I was at my 12th standard. At that time Aunt Mohini used to visit my village frequently, so uncle Ram and I used to stay at home. Till that day I felt uncle Ram was a nice person. That day when I was sweeping the floor, I saw he was observing me. But this time the look was different. When I'm bending, his eyes started watching my breasts cleavage and when I saw him, he just turned his eyes somewhere. I couldn't believe who I thought was my next father had something lusty thoughts on me! This continued for the next few months, in fact it increased more. One night when my aunt was not there he came to my room and started touching me.

I felt uncomfortable and started pushing him, but he was still coming close to me, so I ran out of the room and locked the door from outside and kept the sofa behind the door and stayed crying for the whole night. The next morning the sun shone bright, taking away a bit of the chill. I cleaned the whole hall and replaced the sofa in the right place and unlocked the door and went early to my school.

The evening when I saw Aunt Mohini, I hugged her and started crying, she asked me what happened! But I didn't say anything and stayed calm. I said I missed you aunt!

Oh really! So sad beta. I'll never leave you again she said.

Sunitha shouted Wow! Look how beautiful you are and startling back to reality I reminded myself that I'm not in such trouble and I'm in my marriage looking for a better future.

Few relatives, Mohini aunty and Sunitha took me to the stage I can hear a voice beside me who is talking on the phone very angrily, I turned my head and saw him. He was Hemanth, my future husband probably in the next couple of hours. He saw me and came to me and stood beside me.

The cameraman came closer to us to grab a picture of or both.

Hey! Is everything fine? I spoke.

Yes Yes! he said and smiled.

I smiled and remained calm.

I really don't know what he was thinking of me in his mind. He just smiles whenever he sees me. He always remains silent. Last month when I saw him for the first time, he kept calm and didn't talk to me. The same thing happened when we got engaged. I thought he was kind of a shy person who is shy when talking to girls. But the same thing is happening now! ***Arey yar! We are going to marry and we would obviously have sex tomorrow at our first night come on speak anything to me! Why were you shy talking to me? I'm your wife.*** My inner voice shouted.

After an awkward silence for twenty minutes and posing to the cameraman I took a high breath and said, we are going to get married, are you excited?

He saw me and smiled once again...and his phone rang,

Excuse me, he said and left that place. I saw uncle ram is doing the arrangements and my father was receiving the guests.

Hello you look so beautiful my dear, A woman in her early fifties with golden spectacles came to me. She was Hemanth's mother named Vani. She looks fat and she has an old woman look.

I bent down to touch her feet, she took me up and kissed on my forehead but I focused more on Hemanth, he was shouting and looked more frustrated while talking on the phone. I haven't seen that character from Hemanth. Because he always smiles at me and remains silent.

Aunt Shalini had just left when Hemanth came up behind me.

Is everything Ok hemanth? I asked.

He nodded his head but didn't talk.

The guests started coming to take a picture with us...This happened for 1-2hrs long. While every guest took the pictures and left Aunt Mohini came to me and spoke

Beta go to room and take some beauty sleep,

Ok Aunty!

While I was leaving, I felt a tap on my shoulder. I turned around. It was Hemanth.

Yes Hemanth!

Indhu..I wanted to tell you something.

Yeah sure, tell me Hemanth is everything Ok?.

Noo Indhu I was struggling to tell you this for the past 10 days,...I'm in a relationship with another girl. I.. I.. I don't want to marry you!.

What? Come again hemanth.

Yes, Indhu I don't want to marry you!. I'm sorry!

My face color changed. I had never been so embarrassed in my life. Sunitha, who was standing beside me, listened to us and was shocked.

I told Sunitha to go away from us to talk Privately.

We were standing in the middle of the stage and I asked why didn't you tell me about this till now? Have you seen the guests around us...Ok leave about the guests what about me? Look at my father..Do you know how it'll be for a bride's father to listen to this?

I have been thinking about it for many days. Weeks, actually Indhu.

'Really? And you didn't discuss it with me?'My family is here. Their reputation is important. I said angrily in a low voice.

He remained quiet.I don't know what's running in my mind. I just stood silent and my tears started rolling out of my eyes. I wiped them with a tissue.

Hemanth Please let's sit and discuss in the room. I said.

There is nothing to discuss about this Indhu, He shouted loudly and angrily. He shouted as loudly as the matter conveyed to all the guests and relatives in the hall like a perfect gunshot.

I started crying, Sunitha and Mohini aunty came to me.

Hemanth placed his hand on mine. 'Don't cry,' he said this time with a low voice.

Don't make me cry and then say don't cry I said angrily.

Everyone looked at us. I lowered my face in embarrassment. I rushed to my room, shut the door hard and locked. I took my jewelry from my neck and threw it away. I sat on the bed but didn't cry. But the most annoying thing is my thoughts. How can a half married bride and her family face society when her marriage breaks down at the last moment? I heard some sound, it was Sunitha and Mohini aunt banging my room's door. I think they were worried about me!. I went to the washroom , washed my face and opened the door. When I opened the door I saw Mohini aunt, sunitha, Uncle ram and my father worried about me. I went to my father and hugged him tightly and said Dad lets go to our home! I don't want to stay here and cried heavily.

He took me straight to his car and drove to the hotel room.

TWO
CHAPTER-2

No, this is not just a nightmare. I didn't sleep all night so I am imagining all this. I sat on the bed and stared at the empty closet. Then I cried. And cried. Till my eyes were empty.

My inner voice said

"Crying is no use ,
Oh hurting heart..
Oh Dying heart.....
Oh broken heart...
go to sleep ".

The next morning I woke up late, the sunlight which sneaked from the window fell on my face. I woke up and sat on my bed. I didn't do anything, I just sat and thought about yesterday. I know it's hard to forget the bad things. I sat for ten long minutes and then I heard a bell sound. I went and opened the door. It's my father. He came inside and closed the door. He sat beside me , came closer and kissed my forehead and said Don't worry beta! Nothing happened. Just forget it.

"I know dad I'm not feeling for me ! My worry is all about you. How do you face society? How do they look at you? " my

inner voice replied.

Beta! Go get ready! We are checking out the hotel today!. He said with a low voice.

Dad….How are you? I asked.

I'm fine beta! He said and turned around without showing his face.

I went close to him, I noticed he was crying and I hugged him from the backside. When I hugged him, he wasn't able to control his cry anymore and started crying and screaming heavily. I wasn't able to see my father's cry. After a few minutes he remained calm and told me to get ready and left that place.

I freshened up in 20minutes, dressed up, packed my suitcase and went outside.

When I went outside, I saw guests checking out their rooms and standing in the lobby. I went to the lobby, Everyone was staring at me. It's hard to describe the looks that they were seeing at me. I passed them and went straight to the car. My father took my luggage and kept it in the trunk of the taxi and I stepped in the taxi. The driver raised the accelerator and moved the car at jet speed.

The taxi passed through the Sarangi Bus Stop where I had to climb my bus when I was studying. Well, it's the only road to my college and one must go that way. I look out of the window of my taxi, to catch a glimpse of the bus stop. Everything in the bus stop has been changed a lot. It jerked me upright in my seat. As the years go by, my visits to this city are few. As the taxi sped on. On my way back, I decided I would look again. But it was as though a part of my life had come to an abrupt end; a part that I had almost come to take for granted. The link between youth and middle-age, the bridge that spanned that gap, had suddenly been swept away.

"Sarangi Bus Stop" in Hyderabad is not just a Bus Stop for me, it's a place where I learnt how to live. It's a place where I got my first job.

This glimpse of the bus stop took me back to 3years when I was pursuing my Graduation in my final year.

<<3 YEARS BEFORE>>

<<Radio Chants>>
Good Morning Hyderabad.
You are listening to the Indigo Radio 91.9

The temperature in the city is about 22C and the weather is just beautiful.

This is "RJ VIRAJ" with you and the program name is Morning coffee with a stranger.

To all those people who were new to city here

Welcome to the city.

This is the land where your dreams come true.

<<Radio Chants>>

Good Morning Viraj, I said to myself, taking out my earphones from my ears, standing at the 75feet road Sarangi Bus stop with Sunitha beside me and waiting for the 14B bus which takes me to my college.

The Sarangi bus stop was the usual unexciting swamp of churned-up mud, with a tea stall, and several stray dogs and pigs nosing about in a garbage heap.

The Name of the bus stop came from an Italian musician whose name is Sammy. He came to India in his early twenty. He was famous for his instrument which is Sarangi also called Saran or Saranga. This instrument is a short necked fiddle, particularly used for folk and classical hindustani music. After his death, the colony members paid some respect to him and named the colony as Sarangi.

In Sarangi Nagar, there is a clock tower. And like most clocks in clock

towers, this one works in fits and starts: listless in summer, sluggish during the monsoon, stopping altogether when it snows in January. Almost every year the tall brick structure gets a coat of paint. It was pink last year. Now it's a livid purple.

From the clock tower at one end to the mule sheds at the other, this old Sarangi bazaar is a mile long. The tall, shaky three-storey buildings cling to the Complex side, shutting out the sunlight. They are even shakier now that heavy trucks have started rumbling down the narrow street, originally made for nothing heavier than a rickshaw and City Buses.

The street is narrow and damp, retaining all the bazaar smells—sweetmeats frying,

smoke from wood or charcoal fires, the sweat and urine of mules, petrol fumes, all

These mingle with the smell of mist and old buildings and distant pines.

What a voice Viraj has!. Such a beautiful voice I said.

Yes! He has a beautiful voice. Well of course he looks Hot too..

Shut up Sunitha!

Why Shutup? Indhu? He really looks Hot. If I had a chance of meeting him I would obviously ask him to have a date with me.

Ok..Ok..fine leave it!.

How was your internship going on? I asked Sunitha!.

Don't try to change the topic, whenever I talk about Viraj, I look at your expressions, They change a lot. Come one Indhu tell me what's the matter?

I haven't replied to her, But I just hung around, smiling in my most appealing way.

Well of course, Mine was not always a dull life. I had certain perfect figures which made my body look attractive to men. As a young girl, I was beautiful; in middle age I was colorful to boys with a 34 bust size and 36 hip size.

Boys do often have crush on girls, Well , I had a crush on some boys and one of the boys in that list is Viraj.

Viraj was about twenty-five and he looked easy-going, kind, and a simple enough guy who looks Hot in his outfits and works as a Radio Jockey in 91.9 FM radio. He lives opposite to Mohini Aunt's house. I know him by looks but never dared to talk.

Sunitha taped my back and said,

Come Indhu the bus is coming.

The most annoying thing in my journey to the college is that 14B bus. There is only one bus, which is 8AM in the morning and 4PM in the evening. It is an old bus. It never came on time and never reached it on time. The bus noise was rattled by its nuts and bolts and shaky chassis, every part in the bus seemed alive and complaining. The bus moves off of its own volition and whenever there are bumps on the road the bus stops for a few minutes., and the conductor just had time to get on and collect our tickets and sit in his special chair. Most of the passengers in the bus were rural folk. They smoked bidis or chewed paan, shooting the coloured spittle out of the open windows; and, seeing my watch, asking me the time every few minutes. But the conductor does nothing even though they smoke in the bus.

■

After going to college, I saw my schedule.

My Counselor said that today it'll be a guest lecture for the Training and Placement. Sunitha and I went to the Seminar hall and settled ourselves.

'Open the Deadlock Concept,' said Salman, a senior consultant who looked like a rich grandfather in his gold spectacles. His company took great pride in his Thirty five years of service.

I have heard about him in the newspapers. But this is the first time that I was seeing him lively.

Salman always connects subjects to real life incidents to understand the topic quickly.

Deadlock?? This is not an operating system class right? Sunitha said to me.

Well. I don't know. Let's see what he's gonna say. I replied.

'Deadlock Principles,' Salman said. 'Read that line in the principles. That's where employees in MNC who have a lack of knowledge get stuck .'

The basic definition of deadlock is, It is a situation that occurs in OS when any process enters a waiting state because another waiting process is holding the demanded resource.

So this means whenever you have to do anything, just do with your ease and never tackle your life to destruction, so then you'll be the demanded resource and never will be in a waiting position.

To explain this concept in reality,as I always say to my students "Never lead your life to get inconsistency, else you may be stuck in DEADLOCK state for your whole time". Mastering this subject may make your pay-off even better in your MNC's.

'Everyone works hard at the MNC's, there's no exception. If you want an easy life, look elsewhere,' Salman said.

He also said we are going to offer 350 jobs for an Associate trainee in my company if you have a detailed knowledge on Data Structures and Algorithms.

You'll have the interviews from next monday.

Everyone in the room,boosted with some power and nodded their heads confidently.

Thank You Everyone, Will see you on interview day! Said Salman and left the seminar hall.

■

Knowledge on Data Structures and Algorithms? Shouted Sunitha to me while we were walking to the library.

Why not? Every MNC employee should master these topics!! I replied.

Oh Come on Indhu, who had knowledge in those subjects when we were in this college. If I'm not wrong, our lectures don't have much knowledge on these subjects.

Well, I agree with you! But we have to make sure that we gain some basic knowledge on these subjects.

Hmm, Yes we have very less time.

So, tell me sunitha when do we have an interview?

As salman said we'll have it on Monday!. i.e., 28th of this month.

Oh, my god this 28th?

Yes !

What's wrong?

This 28th I have to attend the Writings and Art museum. You know right! From how many months I was waiting for this event.

Don't worry yar! The museum starts at 6PM in the evening and our interviews will close by then. There is a lot of time.

While entering the library I asked What if the interview sessions were late?

Oh my goddd....Did you see it Indhu?

What, what happened?

Look at the shelves! There are no books left. All the racks were empty. She said,

Where are the books?

How would I know?

I think students took all the Data structures and Algorithms books.

Holy Shit!! What to do now Sunitha.

Are we late to the library? Indhu.

No, we were fast but the students were too fast compared to us. As the news came out in less than 15min the books in the racks were empty.

Haha tell them they are books not hot Cakes!

Hot cakes?

Well then Hot chapatis

Indhu what to do now?

Hmm, here is where a smart fellow like us comes in! Let's go home and start watching youtube for the tutorials, so that It'll be easy for us to understand the topic very quickly rather than studying big big text books.

What do you call Sunitha?

Perfect Indhu!.

THREE
CHAPTER-3

Which sorting algorithm has the lowest time complexity? Sunitha asked me when I was rolling my saree.

Heap sort? I answered and looked curiously at sunitha.

Yes it is!.

Uff..,

So how was the saree? I asked

It's nice! Baby. Don't think too much. It's just an interview, not your marriage .

Yea, I know it! Don't remind me all the time and link everything with my marriage. To be honest I still have lots of time to get married. If you are anxious about the marriage you do it!

Well, I'll do it, when the time comes.

Yes, that's the correct question you asked to her Sunitha, started Mohini Aunty!

Indhu Beta, you have to get married soon and give me a baby, I'll play with them.

Come on..Come on Let's end this topic for now, I've to attend the interview now. Let me think peacefully, I said and saw the time and left that place.

I went to the drawing room(where people sometimes call it the Hall/Living room) and turned on the radio.

<<Radio Chants>>

Hello folks,

A very good morning to everyone,

You are listening to the Indigo Radio 91.9

This is "RJ VIRAJ" with you and the program name is Morning coffee with a stranger.

As today is Monday, Most of the people start their new life on Monday whether it is an employee who joins an organization or a teacher who starts teaching a new chapter.

So for them Let me give you a small motivation, as we say in Monday Motivation Quotes.

"When your dream is in your head then destiny is in your hand".

So people who are starting their new life, Let me tell you ALL THE BEST.

Now listen to this super hit song for some relaxation .

<<Radio Chants>>

Thankyou Viraj, I whispered in my mind and turned off the radio.

Indhu, It's been late, come fast, shouted Sunitha.

Yes, coming.

Before I was leaving, Aunt Mohini came to me and said "All the best beta" and hugged me.

Thank you Aunty I said and continued, Aunty it'll be little late today in the evening for me

Why beta?

I'm going to the museum after my interview.

Ok, But don't be too late. She said and then I left from that place.

■

There was a huge crowd at the placement cell. Sunitha's interview was in another block so she went there. I sat on a chair and started checking all my documents and certificates from my file. After some time, the secretary called me to stand before the door. I stood beside the door and felt fear.

Later a bell rang and the secretary told me to go inside the room. I knocked the door and said,

'Shall I come in?'

'Yes; Came a voice from inside'.

I opened the door and went inside, I was shocked! Guess why? It's Salman! The one who gave us a guest lecture.

I went straight to him and stood, he offered me to sit.

I sat opposite him!.

'Introduce yourself Mrs.....?'he said and searched for my name in his file.

'Indhumathi Sir'

'Yes, Introduce yourself'

'I started introducing myself and ended in 40 sec'

'Cool Indhu! How are you doing?'Salman said, staring at my profile on his screen. He was trying to relax me before he asked me the questions. He had the magic spreadsheet with all the students' profile's data open on his computer.

"I am good sir" I said and smiled!.

'Your Saree looks Great Indhumathi' he complimented.

'I smiled. But only a little'

After he started throwing at me all the questions one after one about the CS topics and Basic Programming for 15 min. I answered all of them with a confident note.

After 15 min he stopped asking me the questions.

"Your first interview, right?" he asked.

"I nodded".

'How do you think you have done?'

'I guess I gave my best sir,' I said.

"He laughed" and said "Your performance was outstanding and your confidence was perfect".

I was speechless and smiled gently!.

'Indhumathi you're selected"

'Thank You sir' I said but I felt dizzy. I pressed my feet hard on the floor to keep my balance

'Shall we discuss Package'?he said

"Yes sir" I replied!. Anything higher or more than 25 thousand, would make it a rainbow in my sky' I thought inside.

'Your Package will be 5.5LPA'.

'Sorry, how much did you say again? I asked.

'It's 5.5LPA'. Is it clear Indhumathi? He raised his voice and smiled a bit

'Yes sir, It's clear now!.' I replied.

'Perfect' "Congratulations Indhu" here is your offer letter!.

'Thankyou sir" I said and left that place!

I came outside but acted as normal. But Inside my heart , I felt huge relaxation and excitement. Outside, I pretend to be cool, like it was any other day.

■

Sunitha came to me running joyfully, I thought she would also have got a job. She came closer to me and asked

'What's the status?' Indhu

'Got Job!' I replied and waited for her answer.

'Really?' Yes...She shouted and said I too got it.

We both hugged each other and discussed what to do next!.

"What's the plan Indhu?"

'Which plan?'

'Are we leaving home'?

'Well I was thinking about it, should I go straight from here to the museum or should I go home and go'.

'Well it's too early and the museum starts at 6PM in the evening. It's 1.25PM.'

'Well to be honest Sunitha, the saree is too heavy and I can't carry it.'

'So we'll do one thing then, let's go home, take a nap and then go to the museum' what do you say?

'Hmm, that's somewhat tempting.. Ok, perfect. Chalo let's go'.

After going home, I went straight to Mohini Aunt and told the news. She hugged me tight, kissed my forehead and took some sweets from the kitchen, took my offer letter from my hand and kept it in God's place.. I went to my room, closed the door, took my saree, changed my dress and took a nap.

Later, when I woke up at 4.30PM,

That evening, I saw the magic of the monsoon.

I went to the window. There were clouds overhead, dark clouds burgeoning with moisture. Thunder blossomed in the air. The monsoon was going to break that evening. I knew it; the birds knew it; the grass knew it. There was the smell of rain in the air. And the grass, the birds and I responded to this odor with the same sensuous longing.

A large drop of water hit the windowsill, A faint breeze had sprung up, and again I felt the moisture, closer and warmer. Then the rain approached like a dark curtain. The rain started drumming over the balcony of my room. I sat there without moving, letting the rain soak my sticky T-shirt and gritty hair.

After some time, the rain stopped as suddenly as it had begun. The day was dying, and the breeze remained cool and moist. In the brief twilight that followed, I was witness to the great yearly flight of insects into the cool brief freedom of the evening.

As the rain stopped, I texted Sunitha that she was ready or not, but she replied with "I'm not coming to the museum, better you go".

So I took a shever, wore pretty good clothes, rolled my hair like a bun, hung my handbag to my right shoulder and kept my watch to my left wrist.

I straightly went to mohini Aunty,

'Aunt, I'm leaving, it's already late'.

'Ok beta, Take care! Come fast home' she said and I left that place.

LOHIT CHANDU

FOUR
CHAPTER-4

I like art and literature more. I frequently visit Art museums which happen in my city. Well I believe that real museums are places where time is transformed into space. When I visit museums I spend so much time seeing those art and their culture. I go to museums and see a painting someone living in the past has made and I'm completely blown away. The paintings in the museum convey different messages like A romantic painting creates a romantic vibes in your heart, A history painting picture makes you proud about your country and A crime abstract painting hears more ridiculous opinions than anything else in the world.

Yet sometimes one trembling star comes in the clear sky and makes us think that our life is beautiful. That evening one star came to my sky and made my life look more beautiful.

That evening when I entered the museum hall, the room was calm and occupied with very few people. I started visiting all the pictures in the museum. It was always a lovely experience walking around a museum by yourself.

I went to the old classic gramophone and seeing it, I was involved in it then I felt a tap on my shoulder. He was a man with a long kurta upto his knees. His hair was curly. He was not too tall but he was up to me.

'Hey You ,' he paused, 'wonderful.'

'What'?

'Not you my lady, it's the gramophone' he said and smiled smally.

'Oh'. I replied.

'Are you alone here?' he asked.

But I haven't replied.

'Hey lady, I'm talking to you! Are you alone?'

'Yes' I replied and walked to another item.

But he followed me.

'You look beautiful' he said

'Thank you,' I said.

'Well Your dress is lovely too.'

I knew that he was flirting with me. I walked fast, I haven't talked to any stranger boy till now and for your kind information this was the first time I was talking to a stranger boy.

But he still followed me, I was tense, my face was full of sweat. He suddenly caught my hand, and I forcely looked back at him, he pulled me towards him. That was the first time I was seeing a boy so close to me. I saw his eyes, they were beautiful. He took a kerchief from his pocket and raised his hand and cleaned my sweat. It was nice. I was still looking into his eyes. He raised his voice and said

'Hey Lady...Don't be tense. cool '

I took my hand from him and asked

'Why are you following me?'

'Well, I was alone here!. I wanted you to be my partner for this evening! Will you?

'Will you explore the endless halls with masterpieces hanging on the walls?'

'I nodded my head' but smiled a bit.

'Hmm.. you smiled, that means the answer is Yes, I guess.'He said and continued "I was a writer, I came here for an inspiration to my story, but I found You." I would like to travel with you this evening if you give me permission'. He ended.

'Writer? What type of writer'.

'Well! There any types of writers? I don't know any'.

'What is writing?' I asked.

'Writing means sharing, it's part of the human condition to want to share things like thoughts,ideas and opinions' he replied.

For a moment we both started walking

'Will you be my inspiration for my story?' he asked.

'I smiled'

'Let's make memories this evening looking at the memories'.

'You are talking like a writer'

'A writer always talks like a writer'.

'What's your name Mr.Writer'.

'Name?..Why tell names?'

'Then how can I call you?'

'You can call me as you wish' he said and continued 'let's do one thing, let's not share anything personal with each other but let's just enjoy this beautiful evening '.

'Hmm, seems interesting,' I replied.

We both walked and discussed the museum pictures for a few minutes. After we returned back to the exit gate, we saw that there are good signs of rain in the climate.

'Ok, Mr. Writer! I'll go, it's already late!.' I said.

'Acha!. Can I drop you?' he replied.

I haven't replied anything, but he said

'Hey lady, you can trust me'.

'I saw his eyes, I knew he was genuine . That spark in his eyes makes me believe in him.'

'I nodded my head'.

For a second he went to the parking lot and took his bike and stopped beside me. He asked me to sit.

I sat at the back and to be honest, This was the first time I was climbing a bike with a boy who I hardly knew for 1hour.

He started the bike and the engine ran smoothly. We haven't talked much while on the bike so I wanted to stall the conversation with short, boring replies. Awkward silences lead to many interesting things.

Suddenly the cloud bursts, cool, drizzling a little, almost monsoon weather; but it is still too early for the real monsoon.

He stopped the bike at the Sarangi Bus stop, which is hardly 5min drive from there to my home. But the rain was too heavy so he stopped the bike at the bus stop.

There was no one at the bus stop, the climate was so cool, We both stood calm.

'Did you get your story?' I asked Curiously.

'No but I got a character'.

'Do you have a girlfriend?'

'Girlfriend? No, I don't have'

'Why ? You look smart, Talks great and moreover You are a writer'

'A writer doesn't have any girlfriends because he will always be in love with his words and characters," he replied and continued, ``Will you be my girlfriend my lady?'

'What I replied?'

Yes, I'm in mad with you,

I stood silent.

'Hey cool my lady, I was joking'

He took my hand and saw my wrist and said 'you really have a beautiful Wrist make sure you use a chain watch that matches your color'.

'Wrist'.

'Yes!, do you know girls with beautiful wrists look more beautiful in heart.'

'Stop flirting with me' I said.

'I'm not flirting! I'm serious.'

'Tell me! As a boy what would you like to see in girls'

'Do you really want me to answer the question?'

'Yea!I love to see the eyes and wrist of girls.'

'You're different'. I said.

'Have you read The Beauty Myth of women?' he said.

'No, what's that?'

'A landmark feminist book. It talks about how women are culturally bullied into feeling conscious about their looks all the time,' he said.

'Really? Well, to a certain extent it's true,'

The rain stopped, I said I'll go by walking home. It is very close to here.

'Ok' He replied.

The next morning, I woke up and went to the living room. I saw my father sitting on the sofa, next to Ram Murthy Uncle.

I was surprised looking at my father, so I went to him and hugged hard, He kissed on my forehead and asked,

'How are you beta!'.

'I'm good nanna!'

Go and fresh up beta! I'll wait here, There is a lot to talk about.

'OK nanna' I replied and went to my room.

I locked my room's door and undressed myself and went to the washroom for bathing.

I looked at the mirror and thought about last night. About Mr.Writer.

How simple he is, like nature with a pure heart. Why does the episode with him make me feel so connected, even though it's just two people having conversation throughout the whole evening without knowing each other's names. Well I guess, The comfort of sharing Vulnerable side of ourselves makes me connect with him. Is this the beauty of our episode last evening at the museum?

Once you experience it, it'll become part of our life.

I bathed and dressed myself neatly and went to my father.

'Aunty..I'm hungry'.

'2min beta!, the food is ready, put these dishes on the dining table and tell uncle and your dad to come for breakfast'. Mohini Aunty told.

I kept all the dishes at the dining table. In the meantime, my dad and uncle came to the dining table. We all sat together and started eating.

'Congratulations Beta, I'm so happy for your job'. My dad Replied.

'Thankyou Nanna' and I asked 'Nanna, is there anything important?'

'Why beta! Why did you ask like that?'

'No, No normally nanna. If there is anything important only na you'll come to here'.

For most women, it is that time of the month. For my father, it is that time of the week. The time when he goes hysterical on the phone or he comes to me, he wants one thing more than anything else in the world—my marriage.

'Beta! I thought of marrying you this year so I started seeing matches for you' Here are some pictures.

'What Marriage? For me? Nanna I was just starting my career and you wanted me to get married?' I replied.

'Yes beta, it's the age for you to get married'.

'Dad I'm still 21 and I hardly completed my graduation, that's it. End of story'.

'Indhu beta, if we start searching now then you'll get a perfect boy in 1-2 years' Mohini Aunty said.

'Do as your wish' I replied, took my plate and went to the living room.

I took my laptop, logged into Facebook and Instagram Messenger. I started scrolling the news feed..

In the meantime, Sunitha came to me

'Indhu, Tomorrow is our first day at the office. Did you get your things ready?'

'Yes Sunitha' I replied with a low voice.

'What happened baby? Is anything wrong'?

'Not a good day Suni' Leave it.

'Why baby what happened? Come on, tell me.

'Discussion about marriage and here are some pictures'.

She took the pictures from the envelope and started seeing the photos.

'Hey Baby, look this guy is so cute' she said.

I looked at the photo and said 'Was cute!'

'Was'?

'I don't find him cute anymore, Just take down that photo suni'.

After some time she shortlisted some pictures and showed them to me.

'Look at this picture, he was awesome and look at his profile. He was 6 feet, working as HR in an MNC and earns

1.5L per month.'

I saw the profile and photo and said "He was good".

'Just Good?'

'Okay yar Great!. How does it sound?'

'Perfect'. So you finalized him.

'What Finalize?' I just told that he was great .

So that means you have a special interest in him.

She took the guy's photo and ran to my dad and said

'Uncle, good news! Indhu likes him'.

'Really' show me show me Mohini aunt replied.

'Take it Aunty'

'Wow he looks good suni'

Yes aunty.

'What was his name bhayya?' Mohini aunt asked my dad.

'This guy? Wow, perfect. This guy's name is Hemanth'. They are very close to our home too. This guy was so innocent and handsome and they were interested in Indhu. Also they asked me 2-3 times about this.

'Jai matha, let my child be safe there'. Mohini Aunty said.

'Aunt it's too early for celebration'.

'Dad I'll be doing my job even after my marriage. If that is Ok for those then I'll marry him'. I said bravely.

'Beta they told me that you can do whatever you want after your marriage whether it is a job or studies that is completely up to you.'

'So finally my baby's wedding is fixed' Sunitha shouted.

'Suni shut up! Come let's go and fix our things for tomorrow's office'.

FIVE

CHAPTER-5

This is your desk, said Meena, a secretary of Saleem. 'Look outside, you even have a beautiful Mountain view.' It took me a while to adjust to my new surroundings. My company in that building is located on the tenth to the Sixteen floors. They deployed me to the Winran Server Team which is basically a Networking side. The Winran Server team operates on more than 2,00,000 servers every month. They used to do some patching work to the servers.

'A company broker will call you. To help with the laptop and some necessary items,' meena continued. 'And here are some other helpful contacts.'

She gave me a file of all the people who would help me. And she told me that Mr. Ramanathan will meet you in his office after 1hour. She said and left that place. Ramanathan was my Reporting Manager.

After some time, A call from the IT dept came regarding the laptop. They told me that a person named Mahinder will come to you and hand you a laptop. After 15minutes Mahinder came to me and handed me the laptop and created an Outlook account for me and handed my ID access card to the company.

I logged into my computer, arranged the stationery on my desk. I put up a few family pictures on my cubicle walls.

I walked up to the Ramanthan office.

'Ah, Indhumathi. Come right on in,' Ramanthan said.

He wore a Black shirt, silver cufflinks and a blue Hermes skinny tie with Cement color Trouser. I haven't seen him during my interview day.

He offered to let me sit. The sunshine pouring into the room made my skin glow.

'Thank you for having me in your group,' I said.

It's our pleasure. He replied and continued 'Did you get your accessories like laptop and ID card right?'

'Yes Ramanathan' I said.

'You can call me Ram' he said.

'Ok ram' I said and left that place.

One month later on the last day of my associate training, I received an email from my Reporting manager, Ramanathan. He had called me to his office. I wondered if I had done anything wrong. I had skipped class to meet Sunitha a few times. Had they found out?

``Good work Indhumathi, your performance was really good," Ramanthan Said.

'Thankyou Ram' I said.

'This is your last day of your training and I'm assigning you to go and join the Patching work team' he said.

'Ok ram'. I said

Most of the freshers dream in the Winserver project is to assign work at Patching, and of course my dream is also to get a place in Patching and Finally I succeeded in it.

The next day, I received a message from an unknown number saying

'Hello'.

I replied with 'Hii, who's this?'

'Hemanth it is' he replied.

At a moment my father phoned me saying,

'Beta I gave your number to Hemanth'.

'Nanna why the hell did you give me my number?' I shouted and punched my cubicle.

'Cool beta, there is a news that I should tell you'

'What' I asked angrily.

``We fixed your engagement on 20th this month and marriage on 29th'.

'Nanna, there is only 10days from now, it's too fast and I have to go shopping and it's too short a time'.

'Yes beta! But on the 29th we have the best muhurtham and if we miss it there is no good day until 3months'.

'Ok nanna' I said and ended the call.

I phoned Sunitha and told her the news; she felt so excited as tomorrow is my marriage.

I completed my training session early and went home. Mohini aunty started preparation for my engagement.

'Aunty, why are you in such a hurry?' I asked.

'Indhu beta! Did you hear that news from your father? Your engagement is on 20th of this month i.e, exactly we were having only 3 days from now' she replied

My inner me thought that ***"Except me, everyone in my family felt excited"***.

I took a shower and went to bed. I closed my eyes. I slept, or passed out, as weeks of sleep deprivation caught up with me.

'Hii' I texted to hemanth in Whatsapp. When I was sitting in the waiting hall at the Beauty Parlor. But there was only a single tick. I opened his display picture and saw the picture. He was wearing a Gray Under Armor T-shirt, with black shorts. He was standing and placed his hand on the edge of a door. I could see his bicep flex through his sleeve in the picture.

I hardly went to beauty parlors only 2-3times in my life, the first time I went to a beauty parlor was with Mohini Aunty, the second time with mohini aunty and the third time with mohini aunty. She does believe that a girl should look handsome and be sexy to the boys, for that she would go anywhere and cross any boundaries .

I opened the whatsapp once again and saw Hemanth's chat. But the message that I sent is still in the single tick. I kept my phone in my bag and in the meantime a beautiful lady with black uniform came to me and asked,

'Hi Miss, How can I help you?'

'Hi, I have my marriage Engagement tomorrow, So I just wanted to make some formalities to my face' I said.

'Ok sure, mam. Just give a minute' she said and went to bring the menu card from the reception desk.

She took a couple of minutes and came to me with the menu card.

'Mam here is the menu, we have shortlisted the menu for the different categories and here is the engagement menu for a bride. '

'Ok..give me sometime, I'll be back with you' I said .

'Ok mam sure. Have your time.'

I opened the menu card and saw it. To be honest I don't know anything in the menu list. I spent some time by watching that menu card and called the lady,

'Hi mam' She said.

'Hi, To be honest I don't know anything about these things in the menu card' I said'

" I believe that, if you have no clue of what to do, best to surrender".

'Oh..That's not a problem mam. I'm here to help you,' the lady said and took me to the next room.

She offered to sit in the chair opposite to the concave mirror. She said we are having a package for the upcoming marriage ladies which include Facial, Threading for eyebrows, Honey Waxing to the arms, legs and thighs for just 499 INR.

'Ok fix this package'. I said and continued 'How much time does it take for all these'?

'It's only 3hrs mam.' she said.

She adjusted my chair,took a cloth from the desk and placed it on me. She took my handbag from me and kept aside.

She cleaned my face with some oil and placed a white strip of cloth on my face and closed my eyes with two eye shaped cucumbers.

After sometime the lady asked me to take my pants and sit with underwear. She took a cup of honey and washed my thighs to legs completely for 15min and later She applied

the wax on my upper thigh, then put a white strip of cloth, six inches long and

two inches wide. The hair from my leg clung to it. I felt relaxed and suddenly she took the cloth with a speed.

'Oh Oh... Slower, it's hurting,' I shouted loudly to the lady.

'Relax Madam' It's over. She said,

She finished my legs from the front and flipped me around. I felt like a fish being scaled before dinner.

Tears started rolling out from my eyes. She gave me some tissues to clean my tears After she asked me to dress up.

She then took some threads and placed it on my eyebrows. And the same thing repeated once again , I started shouting, oh oh.. Slower and she said Relax Mam. It continued for the next 30 minutes.

After everything was over, She took me to the mirror. I saw myself in the mirror. I felt I was completely new this time. Feeling pain for a few hours is not a big task for looking beautiful, I thought .

I swiped my credit card and paid the bill.

I took my mobile from my hand bag, I saw 3missed calls from hemanth. I opened his Whatsapp chat and I found a few messages from him.

So I opened it curiously and saw those. "Hi Indhu, Can I call.?" it is.

I texted with "Yes".

My phone rang.

I picked it up.

'Hey,' Hemanth said. ***"I had started to recognize his voice, That's a good sign, isn't it?"*** I asked myself.

I took a few seconds to respond to him, and said 'Hi, Hemanth. All good?'.

"Yes, all good here" he said and continued "Indhu, let me get it straight to you, 'I wish shall we meet once personally,".

I laughed and said 'That's sweet.

'Cool then, Let's meet today at 5.30PM at a Cafe?' he said.

'Sounds good. Done' I said.

'Bye then, see you there Indhu' he said and hung up the call.

I went to my home, I saw my dad, Ram Uncle sitting in the chair and discussing the engagement function.

'Where is Mohini Aunty?' I asked.

'Sunitha and Mohini went to the market,' Ram Uncle replied.

I went straight to my room, opened my wardrobe and took the best dress to wear. I took my face wash and cleaned my face. I undressed myself and looked at my legs. The wax worked really well. "I looked very sexy" . Even the wax involved pain, it showed me sexy now.

I cleaned my legs, wore pretty clothes and inserted the best perfume on me and started to go. I opened my room door, I saw suni and Mohini aunty came. As I walked,

'Where are you going beta!' Aunty asked.

'Just to meet a friend' I replied.

'Beta....You have an engagement in 2days and you are roaming outside, the weather is too hot. Go take some rest and make yourself more beautiful for that day'. She said,

'I was going to meet your Mr. Hemanth' I thought to myself.

'No aunty!. Only for today.' I said.

'Ok beta!. No more meetings from tomorrow,' She said.

'Ok' I said and went outside to wear my Chappels.

While I was wearing my chappels, I felt a tap on my shoulder. I turned around and saw it's Suni.

'Indhu, tell me where are you going'. She asked

'To meet Hemanth' I said in a Husky voice and ran away.

Later I sat on the bus and texted Hemanth

'I'm on my way to the cafe'.

'Yea...I too If you reach early sit at table no 15. ' he texted back.

I took Suni's chat and texted her 'Not to tell anyone in the house about this meeting with Hemanth' and she replied with "Thumbs Up symbol".

I entered the cafe.The plush cafe and lounge had decadent leather sofas and dim lighting. "How can I help you Mam" A waiter with a white shirt and black coat asked me.

"Well, I had a reservation with table number 15" I said.

"Ok mam, let me check once" he said and continued "Is the reservation name is hemanth?

"Yeah" I said.

``Yes mam, please follow me" he said and took me to table number 15.

`` I sat on the sofa and waited for him for 5long minutes". There is a big mirror beside me and I can see the road from that mirror.

" I saw him coming from the mirror. He parked his car at the parking lot and opened the car door and talked with somebody." Maybe his friends were there in the car I thought.

He entered the cafe and moved around the cafe and stopped right next to me. He had great perfume on, the kind that makes you want to go closer and smell it some more.

He sat opposite to me, he took his goggles from his eyes and placed them on the table.

'What should I tell now?', 'Should I start the conversation?' I asked myself. I took a long breath

'Nice place,' I said

'Yeah..it is' He replied.

'So how was your day?' I asked.

``Good, we are building an application so that's why late," he said.

'No worries' I said.

The waiter came to us and asked

'Sir, Order please'. He handed over the menu card to hemanth. Hemanth gave the menu card to me and asked me to order. I saw the menu card, the rates were high... I took a few seconds and ordered "Pancakes with Lemon Juice" and I asked hemanth to order for himself.

He hadn't seen the menu card and ordered Cappuccino. The waiter took the order and left that place.

Hemanth looked into my eyes. He did have a philosopher look about him, with his beard and uncombed hair and his perfume was top notch.

'You look,' he paused, 'wonderful.'

'Thank you,' I said.

'Is there anyone in the car?' I asked.

'Yeah... Shalani is there!'

'Shalani?'

'Yea...my friend.' he said and continued 'Indhu I need to talk to you' suddenly his phone rang.

He lifted the call and talked for 1-2 minutes,came to me and said I have to go. It's an emergency!.

He paid the bill and left that place.

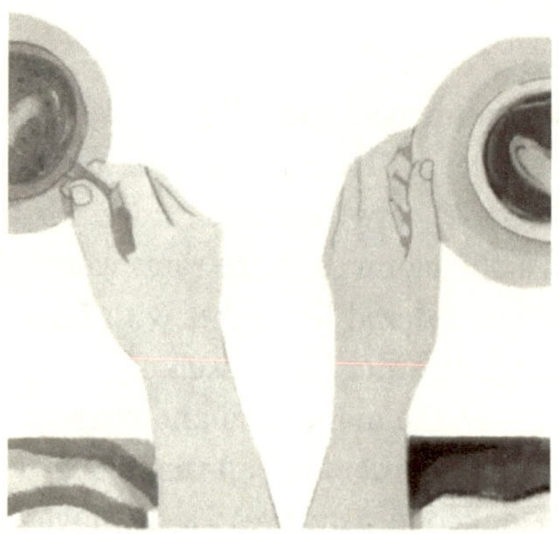

SIX
CHAPTER-6

'How is he?' Asked sunitha.

'Why were you so excited, Suni? He was my hubby?' I said.

'Oh, Hubby'

'Yes'

'Tell me, what does he look like, does he have a body?'.

I opened his profile picture and showed her his picture. 'Oh, my god did you see that bicep, Indhu? He has a gym body,' Suni said.

'Yea' I nodded my head.

``Lucky girl, So tell me how was your first meeting'? Suni asked curiously .

'Do you know suni, he smells nice! I like people who smell nice'

'I hate smelly people'

'Really? Why?'

'So you like smelly people?'

'Everyone has a different smell... that's how people get attracted to each other'

'So, he smells nice right?' Suni said.

'His perfume was so much attractive suni' and 'Everything is fine with him, we haven't talked much but he came with his friend '

'Friend?'

'Yea'

'Girl or boy?'

'Girl...I haven't seen her. She was sitting in the car and her name is Shalini'

'Shalini...Something is fishy Indhu'.

'Shut Up suni, He told me that he wanted to tell me something but suddenly he got a call so he left.'

'Then call now and ask him'

'Now..it's 11.30PM'

'No problem Indhu call him'.

'Not now suni' Off the light lets sleep. I said.

Mohini Aunty had spent the last two hours changing in and out of a dozen dresses for me. Finally, she took the green one and gave it to me to wear.

'Is it showing too much cleavage?'I said.

'No beta!' It's perfectly alright. Get ready fast. The time is running out. Sunitha beta! Please try to put on some makeup for Indhu! She said and left.

She took the mascara from the makeup kit and applied it to my eyes,later took lipstick and kept it to my lips.

'The lipstick is too heavy, Suni '. I shouted.

'Oh god...' she took a tissue from the dressing table and wiped some of it'.

My dad came inside and said, beta! The car came, shall we move? The boy's side has already started.

'Yes dad' I'm almost done'

'Beta, you look the same as your mother' he said and took me to the Mother's photo and asked me to pray for the wishes.

I folded my hands and closed my eyes and prayed to my mother's photo.

Mohini aunty came to me and kept some dark black dot on my ear backside and kissed my forehead.

I hugged her and went to the car.

After 15minutes we reached the banquet hall. The boy's family had already arrived.

Mohini Aunty and Sunitha took me to the stage and a voice came saying

``Hello you look so beautiful my dear, A woman in her early fifties with golden spectacles came to me. She was Hemanth's mother named Vani. She looks fat and she has an old woman look.

As she was short, She raised her legs and kissed me on my forehead.

Later I felt some nice smell from beside me, I turned my head and saw it was Hemanth. He wore white shirt with Dark Green Coat outside, silver cufflinks and a Dark green Hermes skinny tie. He looked at me and smiled. I smiled back at him.

Later the photographers came and took some couple pose pictures, after that we exchanged our rings.

After that both the boy's family and my family came together for a group family picture and then after Photographer asked Hemanth to catch my back waist look into her eyes to grab a picture.

He touched my waist and it felt like magic to me, he looked into my eyes and it passed like a high voltage current and I looked into his eyes then the photographer grabbed a picture of us.

Before my marriage day evening when I was watering my plants on my dhaba, I saw a huge thunder in the sky and clouds loomed up on the horizon growing rapidly into enormous. Then all of sudden a lashing wind swept the rain across my face. The wind blew my hair as it used to...then I started running to my room. I went to the balcony and opened my Whatsapp. There are few messages from Hemanth. I opened them and saw it,

'Hey! Shall we meet?' he texted.

"How can we meet, tomorrow is our marriage and definitely Mohini Aunty will not allow me to go outside" I thought inside.

'Can I call?' I texted him and went to my house. The hall was full of relatives and my cousins surrendered to me. Mohini Aunty and a few relatives asked me to sit near to them and Mohini Aunty is packing my bag for tomorrow's wedding. While I was talking to them My phone buzzed twice. I saw its hemanth.

'Sorry, phone. Maybe dad needs something,' I said and left that place.

'Sure,' They said.

I went upstairs and sat near my plants and saw the lighting stars and dark sky. I lifted the call and said

'Hey!'

'Hii Indhu' hemanth said and continued 'Are you free'

'Yeah' I said in a husky voice.

'What happened, why are you talking like that?' He asked.

'Nothing the house is full of relatives' I said.

'Hmm, Indhu I wanted to tell you something' He said.

'Yeah tell me' I said.

He maintained an awkward silence for 1minute and took a heavy breath which I could hear and said 'Indhu, do you know my friend shalini'?

'Yeah , That day I saw her' I said and continued 'Is anything wrong?' I asked but in meantime Mohini Aunty came to me and shouted

'Beta what are you doing here?'

I hung up the call and said 'Nothing Aunt'.

'Beta what happened? Who is on the phone? ``she asked.

I hesitated for a minute and diverted the topic by saying Aunt when will you apply mehndi to me?

'Oh..beta I forgot..come on fast let's apply mehndi'. She said and left that place.

Later everyone sat beside me, I sat on the sofa and Mohini Aunty came up with a plate of Kaveri Mehandi cones. Everyone took one of the packs and Mohini Aunty took one, kept a small hole for it and started applying it to me. Mohini Aunty was expert in keeping the best designs.

'Aunty, why do we keep mehandi?'. I asked.

'Beta, in olden days our Ancestors came to know that the mehandi paste is a sign of positive spirit and good luck. Mostly in the wedding's it's a tradition to keep the mehndi before the wedding day as a way of wishing the bride good health and prosperity as she makes her journey beautiful.' she said.

The next morning Mohini Aunty and Sunitha woke me up early and asked me to freshen up. I wore my yellow churidar and later all my female relatives came to me and took me to the verandah which was decorated. Yeah it's my haldi function. All the relatives took the yellow paste and applied it to my face and body. Later they took a steel iron tub of water and poured it on me.

Later we went to the banquet hall and the boy's side and my relatives came, I dressed up and my marriage was broken.

<<PRESENT>>

The big blow of the horn startled me back to reality. I reminded myself that my marriage has broken down. I saw the time and it was almost 5 in the evening.

'Where are we'. I asked.

'At the tollgate and 30km to the destination mam'. Driver said.

I opened the window and looked outside, there was a big queue in my line. I opened the door and stepped outside and said meet me on the other side. I took his phone number and saved it in my contact list. I slowly started walking through the road. The marriage breakup Pain still singed my heart. I had told myself to not think of that nightmare.

"Focus on the walk, breathe" I told myself. ***Why doesn't the brain listen once in a while?*** I asked myself.

I crossed the toll gate and went to the other side. I waited a few minutes there for my car. After a few minutes my car came. So, I started walking through my car, then suddenly a lorry came from my backside and crashed into me. I don't know what happened at that moment. I was traveling in the air for almost 10 seconds and fell down hard. The road hitted my head very hard. I can't move my legs and hands. My eyes were blurred and finally I closed my eyes.

The road is full of my blood and people surrounded me.

SEVEN
CHAPTER-7

I started trying to open my eyes. But I was not able to do it. I tried once again to open it. My eyes have been opened small but I can't see anything. It's blurry and my eyelashes were sticky. I tried hard to open my eye lashes, I don't have much strength to open them, I felt weak. Anyhow slowly I opened my eyes.

All my surroundings were equipped with hospital items, I realized that I was in a hospital. The room was dimmed and I felt cool. There at the corner of the room there is a black sofa and I saw a girl sleeping on it. I couldn't see her face. The girl was wearing Red kurta. After seeing her for a few minutes I recognized as Sunitha.

I tried to call her, but my mouth and nose were closed with an oxygen cup. My fingers were clipped, I was covered with a surgical gown and my head is covered with a big white cotton bandage. It may be a skull injury I guessed.

I was able to feel some sense of pain now, the pain is increasing every minute. I can now see everything clearly. I wanted to raise my voice and call Sunitha, but I couldn't because of this oxygen cup. I raised my hand and tried to push the steel table which was beside me, so that she could wake up and come to me.

But I couldn't do it, I felt very weak and my head pain was horrible. I can sense every part of my body....

Wait Wait..What about my legs? I couldn't feel any sense from my legs even from the coolness of the room. What happened to my legs? I felt nothing.

Slowly I tried to push the steel table and succeeded.

That big sound made Sunitha wake up. She switched on the lights and came closer to me. She was shocked to see me wake up and called Doctor.

The doctor and the nurse came to me and checked everything,talked to Sunitha and took my oxygen cup and said

'Hello Indhumathi. How are you feeling?'

'Fine' I said in a low voice.

'Are you able to breathe?'

'Yes doctor'

'Good, you're absolutely fine..Don't worry' he said and left that place. Later Sunitha came to me, sat beside me and catched my hands in her hands and started crying. I wanted to stop her crying but I couldn't do anything.

'How are you baby'? I asked her.

She wiped her tears and said '...I miss you'.

'I miss you too baby' I said and continued 'Where is dad and Aunt'?

'They were at home..they'll come in the morning'. She said,

'What happened to me?'

'Nothing baby..you're absolutely fine..A small head injury that's it' she said. 'But there is something I need to know, I guess.' I replied.

'You are in a coma for 3 Months'. She said,

'Coma?'

'Yes baby...Don't worry..See now you're awake.

'Baby what happened to my legs?'

'Legs......Nothing!'.

'Baby..tell me.' I said.

'There is spinal damage in your spinal cord. There will be therapy sessions for you after that you can walk.'

'That means I cannot walk right?'

'No baby.. You can walk..You'll walk' she said and turned away from me, started wiping tears and continued 'Baby relax for sometime, we can talk morning' she ended and turned off the lights.

Within a few minutes she was asleep. I, on the other hand, kept awake all night, wondering what I could do with the next coming days sitting in a wheelchair.

The next morning, My father, Aunt and Uncle Ram came to the hospital, they saw me and got emotional. We talked for a few minutes and the nurse told me not to get more stressed.

Later the doctor came and gave me discharge. I saw the wheel chair which is kept beside me. My dad took me up from the bed and kept me on the wheel chair and took me to the car. After a few minutes I reached Sarangi Nagar. My colony people came near me to see. I rolled my wheels and went to my bedroom. It was months since I'd last been there. A crisis in my affairs, Accidents and an entire monsoon had over in the hospital and in pain. Now I tramped through late monsoon foliage—which gave me some hope to start my new life like a coloring flowers. I went to the balcony where my plants were planted. When the plants saw me, they made it as if to turn in my direction. A puff of wind came across the valley from the distant Mountains. A long-tailed blue magpie took alarm and flew noisily out of an oak tree. The cicadas were suddenly silent.

But the plants remembered me. They bowed gently in the breeze and beckoned me nearer, welcoming me home.

I went among them and acknowledged their welcome with a touch of my hand against their trunks— the roses are smooth and polished; the pine's patterned and whorled; the oak's rough, gnarled, full of experience. He'd been there longest, and the wind had bent the oak's upper branches and twisted a few, so that it looked shaggy and undistinguished. But like the philosopher who is careless about his dress and appearance, the oak has its secrets, a hidden wisdom. It has learnt the art of survival! A human should always learn how to survive from a plant. My oak tree gave me some hope to survive .

After a week, I was habituated to the wheelchair and the environment. I become less talkative and more readable. I read more than 25 books and planted 67 plants in 7 days. But still there is something haunting me inside whether it is Hemanth or about my legs. One day I opened my laptop and saw all my company mails and phoned Ramanathan and informed about the incident. He gave me 1 year to rest. I was now free and able to concentrate on how I should overcome this.

The trees stand watch over my day-to-day life. They are the guardians of my conscience. I have no one else to answer to, so I eat and read on the balcony and spend most of the time with them.

Sometimes I thought 'What would the plants think of me?' I ask myself on many occasions. 'What would they like me to do?'

Well, it's nice to have someone to turn to..

So finally one day, I realized I wanted to write a Book. Maybe a good reader is always a good writer. I thought that this writing would change my mood swings and turn into a new beginning to my life.

I realized I wanted to write a story about a girl's life. I took a strong core point and started to develop it.

I do nearly all my writing at this window seat of my balcony. The trees watch over me as I write. Whenever I look up, they remind me that they are there. They are my best critics. As long as I am aware of their presence, I can try to avoid the trivial and the banal. After 42 days I completed my script work and published it.

In the journey of writing the book I realized and Sometimes I wonder if I have written too much. One gets into the habit of serving up the same ideas over and over again; with a different sauce perhaps, but still the same ideas, themes, memories, characters. Writers are often chided for repeating themselves.

Don't know whether the book will be a huge success or not, but it definitely changed me. I stopped thinking about my past and about my legs. I was going for the leg therapy sessions. I knew I didn't get my legs back..but still the time taught me to Never Give Up.

The books I wrote got published and I got a huge margin of amount from it. Every girl in the country liked it. One day

I got a call from Times of India for an interview about my book.

I invested that amount in a small business(Boutique) which I wanted to do in my teens. Now I'm an entrepreneur and an Author. One day when I sat at the counter and turned on the radio.

<<Radio Chants>>

Hello folks,

A very good morning to everyone,

You are listening to the Indigo Radio 91.9

This is "RJ VIRAJ" with you and the program name is Morning coffee with a stranger.

As today is Monday, Most of the people start their new life on Monday. So for them Let me give you a small motivation, as we say in Monday Motivation Stories.

There is a girl near my house, whose marriage was broken and her legs were tampered during the accident, but she never lost her hope, she turned herself into an Author. We all know who she is right?

She has been featured in Times of India and her name is "INDHUMATHI" and she was an inspiration for many.

"When your dream is in your head then destiny is in your hand".

So people who are starting their new life take her as an inspiration,

Now listen to this super hit song for some relaxation .

<<Radio Chants>>

That moment I felt proud of myself and sipped a coffee in silence.

I came to Sarangi Nagar at the age of 6 from a village, got sex abused from my own uncle Ram, got marriage breakdown, Got accident, went to coma for 3 months and moreover the pain of no more legs to Keeping a business in

Sarangi Nagar and named as a professional daring lady.

A girl's life is Not yet over if she fails in her studies or if her marriage breaks down. Stop looking at that point. There is a life for every girl even after her marriage breaks down.

Thankyou for reading my story.

This is INDHUMATHI.....Signing OFF.

THE END

About The Author

"*LOHIT CHANDU has been writing for over three years, and has now over 3 titles in print—novels, collections of stories, poetry, essays, anthologies and book. His most recent work is the novel, Indhumathi. His first novel, COLORFUL TALES received lots of appreciation from the readers.*

His second novel is SANJU'S STORY. He recently went interview with GUJRAT'S No.1 PUBLICATIONS and they posted his interview in their magazine.

He was born in 1999 and grew up in Visakhapatnam, Andhra Pradesh. He completed his graduation in Computer Science and Engineering and present working in HCL TECHNOLOGIES."